Esther's Celebration

THE
LATTER-DAY DAUGHTERS
SERIES

Library of Congress Cataloging-in-Publication Data
Williams, Carol Lynch.
Esther's celebration / Carol Lynch Williams.
    p.   cm. — (The Latter-Day daughters series)
Summary: During the Utah statehood celebrations in 1896, Esther, after
being rejected for the lead role in her father's play, finds herself helping the
girl who is chosen for the lead to rise to the occasion.
ISBN 1-56236-507-X
[1. Mormons—Fiction. 2. Friendship—Fiction. 3. Family
life—Utah—Fiction. 4. Utah—Fiction.] I. Title. II. Series.
    PZ7.W65588Es   1996
    [Fic]—dc20   96-6873
                        CIP
                        AC

10 9 8 7 6 5 4 3 2 1

Esther's Celebration

THE
LATTER-DAY DAUGHTERS
SERIES

Carol Lynch Williams

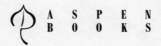

A S P E N
B O O K S

To the entire Aspen staff. I appreciate all you do.
Love, hugs and kisses!

Table of Contents

"I feel to thank God that I have lived to see Utah admitted into the family of states. It is an event that we have looked forward to for a generation."

Wilford Woodruff, 1896

CHAPTER ONE

Discussing Nonny

Things were changing.

It wasn't the fact that the people of Utah were still hoping the territory would become a state, as they had been for my entire life. We knew the President of the United States was looking to make us a part of the country. Nobody was sure when, exactly, it would happen, though my brother and I were practicing a new song with a lot of other children for the celebration.

It wasn't even the fact that I was only Grace's understudy, instead of the lead myself, in the play our neighborhood was performing.

It was because Nonny lived with us now. Nonny, so wise before, so pretty, so perfectly dressed, with just the right memory of everything. Nonny who could remember Joseph Smith, who had traveled all the way from Nauvoo to Utah with her grandfather. My nonny who never complained had changed.

I didn't like it.

"Ethan?" I sat in the study with him while he rehearsed his part in the play. "Nonny is doing it again."

"What's that, Hildy?"

"I'm not Hildy. Be serious."

"It's my line from the play."

"I know that, Ethan."

"Call me Thomas."

"No, Ethan."

"But Hildy, the wind's a blowin'. It's best to run for cover."

I didn't feel a lot of love in my heart for my brother right now.

"Twins," Nonny had told me once when I was eleven, before her sickness, "twins can be very good friends. They are a rare find."

Ha! I had thought, never daring to cross my grandmother. Twins weren't really great friends if half of them was Ethan. He made life nearly impossible by pestering me.

I raised a fist at my brother and shook it close to his nose. He crossed his eyes to look at it.

"Don't worry, Hildy. I'll see after the livestock."

"You think you're the most important twelve-year-old to walk here in the Great Salt Lake Valley, don't you? Just because you got a part in the play."

Ethan bent a little at the waist, like a harsh wind blew on him. "Hurry, Hildy, hurry." He turned, and still bent double, walked out.

"There's been a serious change in wind direction," I called after him.

Ethan stuck his head around the corner. "You're right." He came back into the parlor.

I tried not to smile. I felt a bit snobby. Ethan hadn't realized the wind should have pushed him from the room, and I had.

"I'll do it again," he said.

"No need," I said. "I just pointed out . . ."

"Don't worry, Hildy. I'll see after the livestock." He waited a second for the Hildy who wasn't here, the Hildy that *I* should have been, to answer him. He bent over at the waist again. This time the "wind" came from another direction. "Hurry, Hildy, hurry." Ethan staggered from the room as if a tornado pushed against him.

"Oh, my," I said. I rolled my eyes and followed Ethan out into the carpeted hall. Now he fought the wind up the stairway even though the play, *How the Wind Blew*, didn't even have one stair on the stage at all. Facts be told, most of it took place out-of-doors.

I went to the end of the hall and looked out the pretty stained-glass window next to our front door. The day was cold but sunny. The two walnut trees in our front yard were bare of leaves. A little snow covered the lawn. At least there had been a bit for Christmas.

Ethan was still being blown around when I turned to look at him.

"Nonny always said you and I would be friends," I said. I felt very sorry for myself. Nothing seemed to be going the way I thought it should. Why wouldn't he listen?

Ethan looked over at me. I pretended I didn't see him and heaved a great sigh.

"Nonny will get better," he said.

I shook my head. "I don't think so." I was eager to talk to anyone about Nonny. Even my brother. "She lay on the floor that whole night before we found her."

"We only think she did. No one is sure."

I walked over to the bottom stair and sat on it. Ethan thumped his way down till he sat next to me.

"She will get better," Ethan said. "I promise."

"How do you know?"

"I feel it here, Hildy." He pressed his hand to his heart the way he did in the play. The way he had been doing every minute of the day for the past six weeks. I felt bothered, but I ignored it.

"Do you really feel that way, or are you just acting?"

"I really feel that way . . ." he said, ". . . Hildy."

"Oooo, Ethan!"

"Call me Thomas."

"Be serious just a minute more, won't you?"

Ethan looked around like maybe his audience watched. "For only a minute."

"Promise?"

"Your time has begun. Hurry, Hildy, hurry."

"Forget it, Ethan Wall. I'll have nothing more to do with you." I stood, ready to flounce* from the room. I'm not as good at exits as *some* members of my family.

Ethan reached up and took hold of my arm. "All right, Esther. No more acting. This is really me."

I looked hard into his bright blue eyes, the only thing about the two of us that said we were twins. Not including our birthday. Mother says she's surprised we were even born at the same time because we look so different. Ethan has brown hair. Mine is a golden color. He has freckles. My skin is clear. His nose is straight and mine has a bump in it.

"Your eyes seem to tell the truth," I said.

Ethan nodded.

I sat back down.

"Nonny's different," I whispered.

"She's sick," Ethan said.

"It's not just that. Her face is different. It sags. That one side, I mean. Not a lot, mind you. Just a tiny bit."

"I haven't noticed."

"Well, I have. Take a good look at her. You'll see

5

it. Her left eye looks sleepy."

"I'll look, but I don't see . . ."

"That's not all, Ethan. She's stopped talking."

My brother nodded. "I know. But the doctor said there's a chance she'll talk again."

"It's been almost a month, and not a word from her."

Ethan's face looked a little worried. He stood beside me and rubbed his hand along the dark, smooth wood of the banister.

"She always talked. She always told stories. You know that."

"Well, I can't remember her ever being quiet."

"It's not right. There's something wrong. She should be talking. At least trying to talk. But all she does is sit in her room looking out the window, watching snowflakes fall. Or birds fly from tree to tree. She hardly even eats."

"So what do you want me to do? You're saying things I know all about, but now what? Our talking together isn't going to make Nonny better."

"I know." I felt a little sad. "I'm telling you this because she's staring again and it scares me. I want her to be the Nonny that we knew. Wonder if she starts shouting out strange things the way Tilly's granny did. After all that yelling, the next thing she did was die, remember?" I made my voice low.

Ethan brushed his fingers through his light brown hair, something he always does when he feels frustrated. "Do you think she's going to die?"

"Oh, Ethan, I hope not." Grandaddy died when we were eight. All this time later and I still missed him. Nonny couldn't die. Not now.

"If we could only do something," Ethan said.

I stood and looked him right in the eye. "Well, that's it. Why don't we make her better? You and I can do it."

"Make her better? Esther, the doctor can't even do that. He said let her rest and she might improve. Father spent the most money possible hoping to get Nonny strong again."

"I listened outside Nonny's door when the doctor was here, just like you did, Ethan. I heard what he said. Of course he can't help. He doesn't love her the way we do. He doesn't know her the way we do."

"So what makes you think that we can do anything for Nonny?"

"Because we have to." I smiled at my brother. "And anyway, I feel that we can, Hildy." I touched my hand over my heart.

CHAPTER TWO

Mother's Confession

Father planned to produce *How the Wind Blew* on the sixth of January, in the late afternoon. He had written the play and Mother had picked the cast from the neighborhood children.

This all happened in November, before our Thanksgiving celebration. The reason I felt so badly about not getting the part of Hildy was because Mother hadn't chosen me. She did try and explain why she had overlooked her only daughter. It made me feel a tiny bit better.

"Esther," Mother said, the morning before she went in to tell everyone what part they had received. Outside snow was thick on the ground. November was a very cold month. "I've called you in here to talk about something very important."

I bowed my head as humbly as I possibly could. I had done well in the reading. I knew just by looking at Mother's face when I finished. My cheeks turned light pink at the memory of the day before. I sucked in a deep, happy breath.

"Your reading yesterday afternoon was perfect." Mother fidgeted. She played with the pretty pearl buttons that went down the front of her dress. She untucked a lacy handkerchief from her wrist and held it to her nose. Mother is an actress herself, and I could see by these little movements that something big was coming. It didn't look too good. These were the very things she had done on the stage in another of Father's plays, *The Last Day Cometh with a Song*. It was in a scene where she was telling her family au revoir.* She was leaving with a soldier who had ransacked her small town. Mother had played the lead and gotten very good reviews. That was in New York where both she and Father worked as professionals, Mother as an actress and Father as a playwright.

"Mother," I said. I fingered my own buttons. "What are you trying to tell me?"

"Esther, darling." Mother stood and went to the piano. She put her fingertips on the golden wood. Her nails were perfect little ovals. "I've chosen you to be Grace Overly's understudy."

"Understudy?" I gasped. "Oh, Mother." Without meaning to, I began to cry. My tears felt very cool on my cheeks. Probably because my face burned with embarrassment. This wasn't what I expected at all. I thought I'd be chosen. Perhaps I heard her wrong.

"Did you say understudy?"

"Yes."

"Are you teasing me?"

"No, darling."

"Are you punishing me?"

"Oh my, no."

Mother took quick, little steps to me. She knelt at my feet. "Please don't cry."

"I thought you said my reading was good."

"It was a perfect reading." Mother wiped away my tears. I cried all the harder. It was going to be a job to wipe away all the tears I planned to cry.

"Then why didn't you choose me? Why?"

Mother stood. Through my tears, I watched her clasp her hands under her chin.

"Because dear, I do hope you understand, I wanted to give Grace a chance. She and her family live a life that is a little different. Her father is gone."

"Lots of people's fathers are gone."

"But not for the same reason."

"Well, that's not my fault."

Mother's face got a hard look to it. "Of course it's not your fault. It's no child's fault for the way they live. Grace looked so lonely to me. I thought if she got the part, it would make her feel good. I should think that you would be a bit more generous."

I felt stung. And my mother was the bee.

"But her reading . . ." I started.

Mother interrupted. "It was a nice reading. Especially when you consider her family has nothing to do with the stage. And I've made you her understudy. I thought you might help her learn her lines. Show her how to project* her voice. How to move. Really, I thought you could be her friend."

I had made plans to cry very, very hard, but the look on Mother's face stopped me. She wore a tiny bit of a smile. I could see she was hoping for me to do this for her.

"I have so much," Mother said. "I'd like to think that I share a little of what I have."

"But you wouldn't be doing it," I said. "I would."

Mother nodded. "You're right, Esther. I hope, too, that my children will also be willing to share what they have."

I looked around the room and then at my fingernails.

Mother moved back to her chair and sat down. "You could be such a good friend for Grace." There was no acting in Mother's voice now. She meant every word she said.

I smiled a sad smile, letting the tears drip off my chin. Dripping tears can have a good effect, if you let them drop just the right way.

"Oh, Esther," Mother said, noticing. "I hope you understand. And I hope it won't be too hard on you."

"I will be brave, Matilda," I said. It was a line from Father's play *The Last Day Cometh with a Song*. This was the first play they did here in Salt Lake. These had been Mother's dying words. It was a very sad line. All the women in the audience had cried and the men had coughed. I was peeking from off stage and saw the whole thing. Mother received a standing ovation for that performance.

"Thank you, Esther." Mother held her arms out to me. I ran and sat on her lap. I wrapped my arms around her neck. Her blond hair smelled like rose water.

"I love you," she said.

"I love you, too, Mother. And I will help you."

I remembered all this while I waited for Grace to come practice her lines with Ethan and me. The memory made me feel better about not having the part.

I looked out the front window, past the frilly curtains. Grace should be along any minute now.

It was while I was trying to have a good feeling about not having the part that I came up with the idea to help Nonny. It seemed the perfect thing. There was no way in my mind it could not work.

"Let's have Nonny practice with us, Ethan," I said.

He stood on the velvet sofa, gesturing with his arms and mouthing silent words.

12

"Get down," I said. "Mother wouldn't like you standing up there. Go get Nonny."

"Nonny doesn't want to hear the same lines over and over," Ethan said. He jumped onto the flowered carpet. The chandelier rattled.

"How do you know? She might. She was an actress herself, before." I glanced back out the window. "Maybe it will help her mouth to start talking."

"Well, it's worth a try," Ethan said. He left the room and a few minutes later came back with Nonny.

She sat, small, in her wheelchair. That morning I had carefully pinned Nonny's snow-white hair up. Mother helped her get dressed, managing the small buttons and hooks. It wasn't that Nonny was completely helpless, though the buttons were hard for her to manage. It was as if she were too unhappy to do anything. She never laughed anymore. She never smiled. Her blue eyes were watery and sadlooking.

I went to my grandmother and took her bony hand into my own. "Nonny, how are you?" I didn't wait for an answer. "Ethan and I want you to watch us rehearse. Maybe you can tell us what needs to be done differently. Grace is coming by and we're going to work on stage movements. Seeing that you taught

13

Father so much, we thought you should sit in. I want your help."

Nonny looked at me briefly then turned her head and stared out the window. Grace was coming to the door.

"I don't want her to be able to look outside, Ethan. Why don't you turn her this way some." I motioned with my hands where Nonny should sit. "That way she can watch us." I went to get the door for Grace. She hadn't even had a chance to knock when I opened it wide. "Come in, Hildy," I said with a bow. Cold air rushed in.

Grace giggled. "Oh, Esther. You always make me laugh." Her voice was low—almost not there at all.

"We're going to have to work on your projection, Hildy," I said, taking her wraps* and putting them in the parlor.

We went in the front room to perform for Nonny.

CHAPTER THREE

Helping Grace

Grace was easy to make friends with. The hard part was trying to teach her how to talk so everyone would be able to hear her the night of the performance. The three of us went over the most exciting scene so many times I felt nearly sick of it. Like eating sausage day after day, even this good thing started to get old.

"Louder, Hildy," I said. Grace stood across the room from me. "I can barely even hear you. If I can't hear you standing this close, what about the audience?"

"Well," Grace said. She twisted her small white hands in front of her then stepped quickly to where I was.

"Esther," she said, "we need to talk."

I gazed at her, then back at my brother. "Privately?" I asked.

"Yes," Grace said. She looked at Ethan and then at the floor. "I'm a little embarrassed."

"Ethan, would you mind running and getting Nonny some water?"

"What makes you think she needs a drink?"

"Brothers," I said to Grace.

"Believe me, I know what you mean. Lots of brothers live at my place," Grace said.

I turned to Ethan. "Please?"

He started to argue; then he must have changed his mind, because he nodded his head and walked quickly from the room.

Grace linked my arm with hers and moved me as far away from Nonny as she could. We stood near the fireplace, where a small fire crackled.

"I'm worried about the sixth. It's less than a week away. Every time I think of the play, I feel a bit ill. Here." Grace pressed one hand into her stomach to show where her pain was. "This worry even messed up our New Year celebration."

"Pity," I said, thinking how I would have felt had I not been able to join in our party.

Grace nodded. "There was so much good food. I could hardly eat a bite."

"Perhaps you're cinched too tightly," I said.

Ethan came back into the room with a drink. He took it over to Nonny and helped her take tiny sips. After a few moments, he sat on the sofa and waited.

"I thought so, too, but Mama loosened the stays* and I still feel ill."

"Have you eaten something that doesn't agree with you?"

"No." Grace shook her head and her dark ringlets bounced around her shoulders. Looking at her, so tiny and pale with such brown hair, I was envious. But only for a second. "Your hair is like spun gold," Father always tells me. "And your eyes are the color of the Gulf of Mexico." I'd keep my golden hair and borrow one of Mother's wigs if I felt envious again.

"I thought maybe it was food the first time," Grace said. "It happens so often now, I know that it can't be what I'm eating. Besides, Mama is cooking what she always cooks. Nothing new. This has only just begun. I tell you, Esther, it feels as if a bunch of little animals are running through my insides."

I laughed. "Oh, Grace. That's stage fright. It happens to everyone." I leaned toward her. "Except for me, of course." This was true. I have never been nervous before a performance. Nonny used to say it was because acting is in my blood.

"Oh, I wish I were more like you," Grace said, and her bottom lip quivered. "I can't even see myself doing anything this frightening."

A sudden thought went through my head. Why, I could have this part if I wanted it. Then I remembered Mother and her small smile. "You'll do just fine, Grace. I mean, Hildy. Come now. We'll rehearse again. With enough practice, you'll conquer your fear."

"Nonny and I are getting bored," Ethan said.

Grace went back across the room to where we planned for her to enter.

"Lie down, Thomas," I commanded Ethan. He lay back on the sofa, making sure he kept his feet off the cushions. Not even for a rehearsal would Mother let him get away with his shoes on the furniture.

"Enter Hildy."

Grace moved across the floor. She pretended to look about the room. Then she saw Ethan.

"Thomas," she said.

"Louder," I said.

"Thomas," Grace said. This time it was a little louder.

"Louder," I said.

Ethan flapped his arms around a bit.

"You're not a chicken," I said. "Stop all that flapping, Thomas. You're injured. A possible broken back."

Ethan groaned.

"No groaning until your cue," I said.

"That was my cue," Ethan said.

"Wait until Hildy gives you your cue. Again, Hildy. Loud this time."

"Thomas," Grace said.

It was such a pathetic sound. I felt glad I was a bit taller than Grace. It must have given me a better set of projectors.

"Like this," I said. "I'll show you how."

I walked across the room and took Grace's place. She stepped back and watched me.

I looked around the room, and spying Thomas lying on the sofa, I ran forward three small steps.

"Thomas!" I shouted so loudly that Nonny started* in her chair.

"Sorry," I said as I ran past her and fell to my knees near Ethan.

"Oh my," I cried out, my arms reaching heavenward. "My dear, Thomas. What has happened to you?" My voice was quite loud. I noticed, out the corner of my eye, that Nonny was watching me. An audience!

"My dearest friend," I said. "What has happened to you?" I ran my hands up and down Ethan's arm. "You're injured. A possible broken back."

Ethan groaned.

"Louder," I whispered in his ear.

Ethan groaned louder. It was a good groan.

"Thomas," I said. "Is it your back? Can you sit up?"

"Hildy, is that you?"

"You speak, Thomas. Thanks be to heaven, you speak."

Ethan moved his head a bit. "Hildy?"

"And you move," I shouted, throwing my arms up in praise again. That was something Mother did in another one of Father's plays.

"It was the wind," Ethan said. "It picked me up and slung me to the ground. It was ferocious. It was as if it were alive."

"No, Thomas," I said. "Not here. It couldn't have followed us here."

Ethan groaned in pain. "Yes, it has."

I stood and, facing Nonny and Grace, said in a very loud voice, "I will have to warn the others. No one is safe here now."

I dropped my head until my chin very nearly rested on my chest.

Grace began clapping. "Oh, Esther. You are such a gifted actress. I wish I could do that half as well."

I smiled, feeling very pleased with myself. "You shall, Grace. You shall." I was still feeling very much like Hildy. A heroine.

The clock in the hall chimed eight.

"Oh my," Grace said. "Mama will send someone looking for me if I don't hurry home."

"Her coat is in the parlor, Ethan. Why don't you walk her home? It's not far."

Ethan rolled off the sofa and onto the floor. I could see he was feeling pretty good about his performance too. I smiled at him and he grinned back at me. He got up and went in to get Grace's wrap. After a few moments I heard the front door close.

I went over to Nonny.

"Well, Nonny," I said, leaning close to where she sat. "What did you think? Did I do a good job?"

Nonny said nothing.

"I could have played that part so well," I said. I let out a big sigh.

I spun once in the room, throwing my arms out to catch at the air.

"The wind blows with a force only the gods in heaven can tame," I shouted at the chandelier. Then I fell in a heap at Nonny's feet.

There was a soft clapping sound. I looked up at my grandmother. Were her eyes more blue than they had been just a moment before? I wasn't sure.

But I knew she was applauding for me.

CHAPTER FOUR

Plans ꜰoʀ Nonny

The next morning at breakfast, I made my announcement.

Father sat at the head of the table. Mother sat at the corner beside him. This was so they could hold hands. Nonny sat on the other side of Father. Father insisted on feeding her because she could not lift even an empty spoon to her lips. Father would not hear of anyone else feeding his mother.

"I can't help thinking that she may feel humiliated," I heard him say when Nonny came to stay. I listened at the parlor door. It was open a crack. "For all we know, she's in a deep sleep."

"Her eyes are open," Mother said.

Father nodded. "Her eyes are open. But maybe she's sleeping in here." He tapped at his head. "Maybe we need to jostle her awake."

"I think she's too fragile to shake," Mother said, looking at Nonny who was tied in her chair.

"Dear," Father said, and he laughed. "It was just a figure of speech. I mean, we need to let her know she

22

is a part of the family. Then she can feel comfortable here. You know how independent my mother is. Once she snaps out of this . . ."

"If she snaps out of this."

"I want to think she will. I have to think she will. Once she snaps out of this, I want her to never remember even one humiliating thing."

Father insisted the family do most things for his mother, and not someone Nonny didn't know. "Because she has done most things for me," he said.

Mother never argued, so Nonny sat next to Father.

"Rehearsals are going well," I said that morning.

Mother leaned over her plate a bit. "Are they? Are you helping Grace?"

"We both are," said Ethan. His mouth was full of fried egg. A little yolk ran down his chin.

"Wipe your face, Ethan," Mother said. "No need to gulp. It's not good for your constitution."*

Ethan did as Mother said.

Father patiently fed Nonny bites of omelet.

I sipped my hot cocoa. "Grace is doing much better. You'll see in the dress rehearsal tomorrow night."

"I knew you could do it, dear," Mother said.

"I helped, too," Ethan said.

Mother smiled. "I'm sure you did."

Abigail, our maid, brought in a bowl of sausage gravy. I spooned some onto my plate and dipped my biscuit into it.

"And the lot of you will never believe what happened," I said. I made my voice sound as secretive as possible. Only Abigail looked at me. That's one problem with living in a house full of actors. Everybody uses a secretive voice when they want to get your attention.

"Ethan had left to take Grace home . . ."

"They have quite a nice place," Ethan said. "Both wives stay there. Grace was telling me her mother lives in one half of the house and her Auntie lives in the other half with the other children. She has eight brothers all together. Her father is gone a lot of the time. In hiding, she said. She doesn't get to see him much."*

"You interrupted me," I said.

"Excuse, please."

I nodded at Ethan and started on my story again. "I was calling to the heavens. You know the line, Father, 'The wind blows with a force only the gods of heaven can tame.'" I shouted this last part as I had done the night before, throwing my hands high into the air. Everyone was looking at me now. Especially Abigail. She shook her head a little. She probably never has anyone shouting lines from a play at her breakfast table.

"Very well done, Esther," Father said.

"Well, I was better last night because I could crumple to the floor," I said. I sipped at my drink. "I fell at Nonny's feet, at the end of the performance, and guess what happened?"

"I came home?" Ethan asked.

"Don't be silly," I said. "It was very important." I paused and looked around the table. "Any guesses?"

"I already guessed," Ethan said.

"You were wrong. Does anyone else have an idea?"

"Don't make us try to figure it out," Mother said. "Just tell us. I can't bear the suspense."

"Nonny clapped for me."

Father stopped drinking his Mormon tea.* "What?" he asked.

"Nonny clapped for me."

"Are you sure, Esther? Absolutely sure?"

"Yes, Father, I am."

We all looked at Nonny. She gazed at the half-eaten plate of food in front of her.

"Can it be?" Mother asked, to no one in particular.

"Do you think she'd do it again?" Father asked.

"We could see," I said. "If you want, Father."

"At breakfast?" Ethan asked.

Father took the napkin from his lap and laid it near his plate. "Nonny. Did you applaud Esther's performance? Was it splendid last night?"

Nonny looked at her son but said nothing.

"Go ahead, dear," Mother said to me. "Do it now."

"Come help, Ethan," I said. "And Father, turn Nonny so she's looking right at us."

There was plenty of room in front of the china cabinet, so Ethan and I went there. Father pushed Nonny close. Ethan crooked his back a bit, like he was recovering from an injury. I took his hand.

"I'm glad your back is not broken, Thomas," I said. "It is one less worry on my mind."

"There are still others," Ethan said. "Worries swirl about us."

I nodded. "The wind. How it blows. It shrieks as if it were alive."

"Oh, it is alive," Ethan said. He raised one hand and pointed out an imaginary window. "Only something alive could create such destruction."

I pretended to peer out the window, too. Then I made a small circle in front of the dishes, throwing my arms out. I accidentally slapped Ethan.

"Excuse," I said under my breath to him, so no one else could hear. Abigail snickered from her place near the table. I ignored her. "The wind blows with a force only the gods can tame," I shouted. Then I fell at Nonny's feet.

All was quiet in the room. Then, like the night before, I heard clapping. I looked up. It was Nonny.

Father leapt to his feet.

"Bravo!" he shouted. He smacked his hands together, joining in Nonny's applause.

Mother wiped away a tear with her breakfast napkin. "Esther was right," she said. She began to clap, too.

Ethan helped me to my feet. We both bowed. The applause went on for quite awhile, though Abigail would have no part of it and left the room.

Father decided after that, that Nonny would attend all rehearsals, whether on stage or at our home. As long as she was facing the actors and actresses she was always the first to clap.

CHAPTER FIVE

My Embarrassing Moment

We rehearsed enough at our house that soon it seemed all Nonny ever did was watch us. She never had time to sit at the window and gaze out anymore. I say *we* rehearsed, but I never did. I sat beside Nonny and shouted instructions at people like Grace and Ethan.

Our dress rehearsal was on Friday afternoon. The day was beautiful. The air felt crisp and cold. The sun shone, though it didn't give a lot of heat. We met at the small theater where many of Father's plays are produced. Mother says it is an ornate* building, even if it is little. It's just a few streets over from Brigham Street, where we live.

The children from the neighborhood came in and sat down in the small theater room. Everyone dressed in costume. Grace looked very nice in her pretty button-down-the-front shirt and her school-marm* dress. She was a teacher in the play. Even

Ethan looked nice, considering he's my twin and all. Robert was the wind. He wore his father's big, gray suit, stuffed around the belly. Father wanted Robert to look fat. Of course he is a little chubby so that helped plump out his character.

Father climbed up on the stage and after giving everyone a big smile said, "I know you are all as excited as I. Late this afternoon is our dress rehearsal. In just a few days we will be performing *How the Wind Blew* for the whole of Brigham Street, if they feel so inclined as to stop in. I have invited parents, grandparents, teachers, and even the bishop."

A bit of excited talk came from the actors and actresses.

"I would like for you to go through the whole performance without stopping even once. There will only be four people in your audience today, but I want you to act as you've never acted before."

I felt proud to know I was one of the four. I looked at Nonny. She stared at Father. I crossed my fingers that she wouldn't start clapping for him the way she did for me every time I came in the room now. It seemed she always clapped, even when I just wanted to kiss her goodnight and wore only my nightclothes. Abigail thought it was funny. I didn't care. It seemed Nonny got better every day. Before she wouldn't look at anyone. Now she clapped whenever she saw me.

"Everyone please take your places," Father said. "We will begin as soon as you have been announced." Father jumped down from the stage and went to the back row of seats.

Nonny did not clap.

Mother's voice seemed to come from no particular place, but it echoed over the whole room. "*How the Wind Blew,* written by Mr. Steven Wall. Performed by the Brigham Street Acting Company."

Grace came out on the stage then. Her voice was so soft I couldn't even hear her. And there I sat in the front row. Nonny sat next to me, her wheelchair in the aisle.

"Louder," I whispered.

Grace looked out at me and shouted her next two lines. Then it seemed that she slipped into the book she carried. I couldn't hear her at all.

"Hildy," I said, a little louder this time. "We can't hear you."

From the back came the sound of Father clearing his throat. That's something he only does when he's unhappy.

My face turned warm when Grace missed her cue and stood silently for what seemed an eternity. At last I prompted her. For some reason I felt responsible. Hadn't I been tutoring her all along? If things didn't get better I was would have to go up on the stage and help her out.

The first two scenes were awful. Poor Grace couldn't remember anything. The wind blew at the wrong time. Ethan stumbled over three lines. I know, I counted. The people who played the trees all stood in the wrong places. The visiting salesman forgot his suitcase. It was a disaster.

I leaned forward in my chair and called out little things to help everyone along. It seemed the best thing possible. If everyone listened to me, I might be able to save the show.

Suddenly I heard Father's voice come from the back of the room.

"Esther," he said, after I suggested to Grace that she prance lightly across the stage instead of taking tiny steps. "I think you and I need to have a bit of a talk."

Nonny looked at me. Her face seemed tiny and white in her black bonnet. Father had tied Nonny to her chair because Mother feared my grandmother might fall out as she had once before at home. We rigged the ties so that no one could see them. Father hid them beneath the folds of Nonny's skirts.

Father came over to where I sat.

"Yes, Father," I said. I could see Mother watching us both from the side of the stage. She looked a little worried.

"Everyone hold your positions, please," Father said. He knelt at my feet like a man had once knelt at Mother's feet in a play. The man asked Mother to marry him. I didn't think that was what Father planned to do now. Ask me to marry him, I mean. "Darling, we have a bit of a problem here."

I was right about the marrying thing.

"What, Father?"

"You are becoming too loud. I appreciate your suggestions, but we are now polishing up the play. There's no real reason to make changes."

"What changes have I made?" I asked.

"You keep shouting instructions at Hildy."

"You mean Grace, Father?"

Father gripped my hand in his. "Yes, I mean Grace. And others, too."

"I'm only trying to help her as Mother suggested."

"I know that, Esther. But you're carrying it all a bit far. She's doing fine."

"I really think she should prance. It makes her look so . . . oh I don't know. Dignified."

Father bowed his head slightly and drew in a deep breath. His neat, dark mustache turned down into a slight frown. I knew that look.

"Esther, I am the director of this little play. I need you to sit quietly over here. You are confusing the cast. I don't want to have to send you and Nonny home."

I took in a breath. "I thought I was helping. I only meant . . ."

"I know," Father said, and he touched my head when he stood. He took a step back and put his finger to his lips. Then he winked.

Tears filled my eyes and the stage seemed to swim. Father looked soft and squat. The heavy, red velvet curtains seemed to grow. My face had to be the color of a fall apple.

Mother no longer watched me. She stood on the stage beside Grace whispering in her ear.

"Mother's probably telling Grace not to prance," I said. There was no one to hear except Nonny.

Father went to the back of the room. "Let's begin from where we left off. Grace, your line is: It is as if the sun will never shine again."

I knew if I wasn't careful, I would cry. I sat still and pretended that nothing was wrong. My eyes became too full for me to even dare a blink, so I sat wide-eyed and mumbled to myself, "I can't believe he didn't want my help. All my suggestions were good ones."

Two tears escaped. I wiped at them. This was no time to allow anything to drip from my chin.

Nonny reached over. She took my hand in hers and gave it a tiny squeeze. It was so tiny I almost didn't notice.

I looked at my grandmother. Two more tears rolled down my face. With a great effort Nonny wiped them away.

"Oh, Nonny," I said. "I am so glad that you love me." I rested my head on her thin arm. How I wanted to hide my burning cheeks in the folds of her black dress, like the ties were hidden. Instead, I waited quietly on the sidelines, biting my tongue so I wouldn't shout out any helpful little hints to the performers.

And I cried a bit more.

CHAPTER SIX

Exciting Saturday

I stayed angry with my father all that afternoon and into the evening.

"I'm going to make him suffer," I told Nonny, when we came home. "My feelings are still hurt." Every time I thought of Father reprimanding* me so, my face turned red.

Nonny looked at me. I couldn't tell if she was happy or sad by what I said.

"I gave helpful suggestions, Nonny."

She sat quiet.

"And the play was very bad." Not that I remembered the last scene. I felt so embarrassed that I couldn't do anything more than let tears seep out of my eyes and onto the black silk of Nonny's sleeve.

"Father will be very disappointed when he realizes that I plan to never help him with another play again." The thought of not helping my father made a big lump of sadness come into my throat. I would teach him a lesson.

"He will be very lonely," I said.

I was lonely already. Thank goodness I had Nonny to talk to. I wished she could answer. At least she could clap and reach out to me.

I decided to punish Mother and Ethan as well. None of them would *ever* have me around helping them with their lines again.

"That will show them all," I said.

Nonny just looked at me.

I swung this way and that, telling Nonny all my ideas for making my family feel as hurt as I did about being left out and publicly humiliated at the dress rehearsal.

At last, I talked myself dry of things to do. My grandmother still watched me, though I could see she was becoming tired.

"It's almost time for Mother to come and put you to bed, Nonny," I said. I began to loosen the ties that held her in the chair. I worked slowly and carefully. I didn't want to accidentally pinch her, though it would be nearly impossible to pinch anything through all Nonny's clothing.* I knelt beside her chair and worked. When at last she was free, I leaned back a bit.

"Done, Nonny," I said.

She reached her hand out. Gently she touched my cheeks with her fingers. Her skin was cool. I noticed that her hand shook a little.

Nonny opened her mouth as if to say something, but nothing but a breath of air came from her.

I leaned close. "Oh, Nonny. I love you," I said. I looked into her blue eyes. For the first time ever I realized how much Father looked like her. Seeing how they favored one another made me miss him. Did he miss me?

I could hear Mother, Father, and Ethan talking in the dining room. Ethan laughed about something.

"Come, Nonny," I said and pushed her chair ahead of me. Down the hall we went to the dining room, where I found my father and mother watching Ethan. He was acting silly, imitating the mistakes made that afternoon in the rehearsal.

I stood at the door, with Nonny in her chair. I looked at my family and felt a large lump of love grow up in my chest. The sight of them made tears come to my eyes. I was quiet. At first, no one knew we were there. Then after a moment Ethan noticed us. With his chin he pointed to Nonny and me.

"She has returned," he said. Ethan swept at the air with his hand, showing us the way in.

Father smiled and motioned me to him with his fingers.

"Oh, Father," I said. My voice was loud. "I forgive you." I ran to him and threw myself onto his lap.

He laughed and patted my back. "I'm grateful for your forgiveness, Esther, though I'm not sure why I am getting the honor of being forgiven."

"You know." My voice was muffled in his neck. I was crying. "You're forgiven for embarrassing me. At the play rehearsal."

"So that's it. Well, Esther, I forgive you for interrupting the performers."

"Me?" I said pulling back and making my mouth a small O.

"Yes, you." Father squeezed me and I let out a small laugh.

I hugged Father tightly around the neck, letting the tears run down my face and drip off my chin. Ethan wheeled Nonny into the room with us. After a while Father and Mother said that we could pop corn.

I decided that night, after getting ready for bed, that the day had turned out rather nicely. I went to my window and peered between the curtains. A man and woman walked up the street. They huddled close together, probably because it was so cold. Even with the outdoor light I couldn't see who they were. The glow of the lamp was hazy. The air around the glass seemed soft, like the light had become a puff ball.

I sighed and the window near my mouth fogged. I wrote my initials, E. W., in my breath. If I tried hard, I could forget what had happened at rehearsal. I could forget that I wasn't Hildy in the play. Mother was right. Grace was a good friend. I wondered if that meant I was a good friend, too. For sure, I felt happy that I had helped her learn her lines, even if she didn't prance on stage.

The next afternoon, when Mother read to us in the parlor, Father came bursting into the house. In each of his hands he waved a newspaper.

"It's happened," he shouted, "it's happened!"

Mother leapt to her feet, clutching at her throat. Her face turned pale. "What?"

"Nothing to be frightened about, Beverly. This is wonderful news." Father tucked one paper under his arm and read the headlines of the other. "'Utah A State.' It says right here in the *Deseret News*." Father's cheeks were pink from excitement. "Can you believe it, Beverly? And listen to the *Tribune*: 'The Forty-fifth Star Shines Resplendent.' The news came over the telegraph lines this morning." Father took four big steps and crossed the floor to Mother. He swung her around in a circle. Nonny clapped.

"What, Father?" Ethan asked. "What does it mean, the forty-fifth star?"

"We're a state, Ethan," I said. "Utah is the forty-fifth state in our country. That means we have the forty-fifth star on the flag."

"President Woodruff must be thrilled," Father said. "He's been through so much to make this happen."

"The Manifesto is what set things to change," Mother said.

I remembered this. Mother and Father, and lots of other members of the Church, still talked about the Manifesto. It had happened a long time ago, the year Ethan and I turned six. The Manifesto was a revelation that President Woodruff had received. It talked about how members of our church weren't supposed to practice polygamy. Most Mormons agreed that having more than one wife was not right now. They felt to practice polygamy was to break the law. But some still did, though they did it in secret. A few men were in hiding, like Grace's father.

"Do you realize what this could mean?" Father asked. "Those who do not believe as we do will not be trying so hard to crush out Mormonism."

"It bothers me that we came all the way to this desert to be alone, and the government still tries to change us into becoming what they want," Mother said. Her brow wrinkled. "You'd think we could be left in peace."

"This is a good thing, Beverly," Father said. "I feel it here." He tapped on his chest. "And people are excited. Why, when I was picking up the papers, there was talk of parades. We can sit on the front porch and watch if you'd like. The day is perfect."

Mother smiled. "Times are changing. Hopefully this will makes things better for Esther and Ethan."

"If our voice is heard in Washington, it will," Father said. He half-walked, half-danced over to Nonny, who watched from her wheelchair. "Did you hear, Nonny? We are a part of the Union. I think we should celebrate by going to the theater tonight. *The Lottery of Love* is playing. Henry Dixie is supposed to give a fine performance. And the official day of celebration, our inaugural day, will be on Monday. *How the Wind Blew*, will be a play welcoming in change. A new year, a new play, and a new state, what more could we ask?"

Father seemed very pleased.

I wasn't sure how I felt about the whole thing. Being the forty-fifth state was exciting. Getting a new star on the flag was, too. But it was the mention of parades that sounded most fun to me.

CHAPTER SEVEN

A New Era for Utah

After the news of becoming a state spread through the city, the parades began. Father, Mother, Nonny, Ethan, and I sat on our very own front porch for two.

"Abigail," Father said, during the second parade, "I'd like to go on an evening picnic with my family before the theater. Would you please pack a basket for us?"

"A picnic in this weather?" Abigail asked. "Mr. Wall, you'll freeze."

I was surprised, too. Picnics are summer things, when the ground is warm and the air is hot. It wasn't a real cold day, but it wasn't picnic weather either.

"This is a day for celebrating," Father said. "I want to be out with my family. If we bundle up we'll stay warm."

Abigail did as Father told her to. But as we sat on the cold grass, Nonny covered in more blankets than I cared to count, Father said, "Well, the old grouch was right. It is too cold for a picnic."

Ethan and I laughed but Mother gave Father a disapprovingly look. "Some words shouldn't be said in front of women or children."

"Forgive me, my dear," Father said and he laughed, too.

After our freezing picnic we went home to change for the theater. I dressed in my best silks, my dark blue dress. It's my favorite. I like the lace and swirls. I like the way the waist comes in tight like Mother's dresses do. Father says I am a picture of great beauty in that dress, but I wonder. We went to have our photograph made just a few months ago and I wore that very dress. When we got the photograph back I looked angry.

"I wish they had let me smile," I had said to Nonny. She stood in the picture with us, before she got sick.

"When I was a little girl, if you wanted to see what you looked like, you sat for a portrait.* That took a long while. Nothing like having a photograph made today," Nonny said

"Did you get to smile?" I asked.

"We never had the money to have our portraits painted when I was young. It wasn't until I became much older. You had to sit very still then, too."

"Well, it would be worth it if you got to smile," I said.

Now, when I wore my blue dress I made sure that I smiled all the time, everyplace we went. I did not want to appear angry. It just didn't seem ladylike.

At the theater we sat in our usual balcony seats. Father carried Nonny up the stairs, as he always did now that she could not do things for herself. There were a few people at the performance but nowhere near as many as usual. The building wasn't even full.

"Everybody is out celebrating," Mother said. "Probably people will be doing things they shouldn't tonight."

"It's close to the Sabbath," Father said. "I doubt there will be very much drinking. You know the Sunday liquor laws."*

"I do hope they keep peace. Brigham Street can become very noisy when people think there's a cause for celebration." Mother looked worried.

"There is a cause for celebration, my dear. We are a state. And don't forget that we believe in letting people do as they please, as long as it doesn't harm us." When Father smiled, as he did now, even his mustache looked happy.

"No one should celebrate with liquor," Mother said, but she made her voice low, because the play was beginning.

The Lottery of Love ran late. Nonny clapped after every scene.

"A good little play," Father said when we were on our way home. "I did enjoy Mr. Dixie's performance."

"I like your plays much better, Father," I said.

"Why, thank you, Esther."

"Couldn't you just see *How the Wind Blew* being performed on that stage?" I could almost.

"With you as the lead?" Ethan asked, teasing me.

Of course, I thought. "It wouldn't matter who was the lead. It's Father's play, so that means it's good. Haven't we already proved that by letting you play Thomas?"

"Don't quibble,* children," Mother said.

"I liked the fire best of all," said Ethan.

"You would," I said. "I thought that was the scariest part of the day." A small fire had broken out on the roof of the theater as we were leaving. It hadn't taken long to be put out, and even though I didn't want to admit it to Ethan, the fire had been pretty against the dark sky. But it was too dangerous for me to think it was fun.

"It did add a bit of excitement to the evening, didn't it, Ethan?" Father said.

"Ignore the boyish side of them," Mother said to Nonny and me. "Fire fascinates men."

Father laughed and put his arm around Mother.

"Not as much as you fascinate me," he said and he kissed her cheek.

"Always the writer," Mother said, but she smiled, too.

Sunday was cold and the meetings were long. Everyone spoke of a new year and a new era for Utah.

"Hildy," I said when I saw Grace in church. She came up to me.

"I'm having that stage fright again. It's causing pains. Mama is worried about me," she said.

"You'll be fine," I said.

"Just remember that you're my understudy."

I looked closely at Grace. She really was afraid. I took her hand in mine. "What do you mean by that?"

"Oh, Esther," Grace said, and I could see she was close to tears. "You are so much better than I am at the part of Hildy. If I can't do it, I want you to promise me that you will. We can't let the program fail just because I'm frightened."

The thought of being Hildy burned in my mind. It made my stomach jump for joy. It was just what I wanted to do. That and helping Nonny get better were the two most important things in my life right now.

"I'll be there for you, Grace," I said. I went to Mother and Father and sat down. I held Nonny's hand the whole of the meeting. What a wonderful day this had turned out to be.

I would be playing the part of Hildy after all.

CHAPTER EIGHT

The Celebration

Monday morning dawned cold and sunny. The sky was clear. Church bells were ringing and I could hear whistles blowing, too.

I stretched out under my covers and pointed my arms up toward the ceiling. I let out a big breath of air.

"I am going to be Hildy in *How the Wind Blew.*"

A sparkle of excitement tingled in my stomach. I tried not to think how Mother would feel if she knew I wasn't encouraging Grace to play her part.

My covers were thick and comfortable. I snuggled down into them, enjoying the warmth. Enjoying my feelings and secrets.

"Today will be a wonderful day," I said to the ceiling. "I will be the star of the stage."

In my head I could imagine people coming to speak to me after my flawless performance.

"Esther Wall," one pretty girl would say, "you did such a good job playing the part of Hildy."

I would smile, just a bit of a smile, and bow my head.

"Esther Wall." This would be one of the big boys from church. That one cute Arthur who always sits in the back with his huge family. "When you're old enough to go to a dance, I'd be pleased to take you."

"Of course, Arthur. I'd love to."

Mean little Martha Andrews (who really isn't little at all, especially in this dream) would come to me. "Oh, Esther. I am so sorry for the times I pulled your hair in school. You will forgive me, won't you?"

I would consider forgiveness for a moment. "I don't think so, Martha. Maybe on another day. Be sure to ask again later."

The people who would be most proud would be Mother, Father, and Nonny. Well, not Mother, really. But this was my dream. She *would* be happy. Ethan would be sorry he had ever teased me, because in the play I would outshine even him.

There was a knock at the door.

"Miss Esther," said Abigail. "Time to get up."

I hated to leave my warm bed. The air in the room was cold.

At last I leapt out from under the covers and ran to the mirror. I peered at myself. I smiled at me. I winked at me. I puffed my cheeks, folded my hands beneath my chin, looked back over my shoulder at myself, pretended surprise, then fear. "Esther Wall," I said to me, "today will be the best day of your life." I leaned forward and kissed my reflection. Then I hurried to get dressed.

"Breakfast in five minutes," called Abigail from downstairs.

Ethan ran past my door and pounded on it. "You're going to miss the parade, lazy, if you don't hurry."

"The actress of the day does not have to hurry," I said to the door. I kept my voice low. Ethan clattered down the stairs, whooping as he went. With quick steps I went to the wardrobe and chose a dress. Really, I would have to hurry. Since I was pretending anyway, I would pretend that I wasn't rushing about. I washed my face and hands as quickly as I could, even though the water in the basin nearly froze my fingers off. Then I ran downstairs where a fire blazed in the hearth.*

Wheat pancakes waited in stacks on a dish on the table, and large glasses of milk stood next to each blue-and-white plate. A pitcher of maple syrup, that I knew was warmed through, waited next to a platter of sausages. The air in the room smelled delicious. A little like smoke and a lot like food. My stomach growled.

Father and Mother rushed into the room together.

"There's a big day before us," Father said. "We need to eat as quickly as possible if we want to enjoy everything."

Mother smiled. "Relax and enjoy breakfast, Steven." We all stood behind our chairs waiting for Father to say prayer. Then we could sit and begin eating.

"Father in heaven has blessed us with great things already this year," Father said. "I think we should offer thanks." We knelt next to our chairs, except for Nonny, who looked at her hands.

"I hope we won't be thanking Him for too long," said Ethan.

"Ethan," Mother said. Her voice, a warning.

Father began to pray. I listened as long as I could. After a bit, the smell of food and my thoughts of taking the lead in the play got in the way of my hearing the words of the prayer.

"Amen, Esther," Father said in a loud voice.

I jerked my head up. "Amen. Excuse," I said and Ethan laughed.

Father rushed us, but it didn't stop me from enjoying the delicious buttery taste of the pancakes and the spicy flavor of the sausage. I felt my first drink of cold milk go all the way down and cool off my stomach on the inside. It wasn't long before we were on our way to the parade.

A parade to start the day and a performance to end it, I thought. What could be better?

We found a place on the side of the street where we could see everything. The sun shone down. A cold breeze blew. I wrapped my cloak around myself a little tighter. I was glad for my muff.* It kept my fingers warm. And it matched the ones Mother and Nonny wore.

From down the street we could see the parade beginning. A cheer went up. A man on horseback led the group of marchers.

"Look," Father shouted, and he started waving his hat. "The parade marshal is Robert Burton."

Mr. Burton's horse seemed to nod its head at those gathered to celebrate.

"Burton," Father called.

Mr. Burton saw Father and waved to him. His horse pranced sideways. People on the sidelines called out and whistled. Nonny clapped.

"Who is that, Father?" Ethan asked.

"Why, Robert T. Burton. He led the Nauvoo Legion against an army that came into Utah almost forty years ago."

"Doesn't that make him a little old to be riding a horse?" Ethan asked.

"He seems to be doing fine," I said.

Next came two men in uniform carrying a banner between them. It said "Sixteenth United States Infantry." There were lots of troops, all marching behind Burton. And a band, too.

"Did Mr. Burton come up against men like that, Father?" I asked. "And did they have guns?"

"Of course. Guns and swords. So did the Nauvoo Legion," Father said. "These people are from Fort Douglas."

"I wonder if either side had a band forty years ago?"

Ethan stepped out into the road. Nonny reached after him, but she was slow and missed grabbing hold of my brother. Ethan ran up to one of the infantry men and, mimicking him, marched along with the group. I hid my face behind my muff. Why did my twin have to be such a showoff? At last he turned and ran back to where we were. Father didn't even seem worried.

The parade was long. Firemen pulled a hand pump. It was very old and I felt glad the fire Saturday night hadn't had to be put out with it. Bands, different groups of people, and state officials walked down the street. There was even a float with men performing flips on parallel bars.

"Father, we could have done that, with our children's acting company," I said. I imagined a gold banner on our own float that said, "Brigham Street Acting Company."

"If we didn't have our performance today, I would have said yes to the idea."

My stomach flipped thinking about the play. I grinned.

We went home for lunch.

"Children," Mother said, "you need to hurry so we can get to the Tabernacle."

Oh, I thought. Singing in front of everyone. Why, I'd be a star *twice* today.

"I still can't believe they want me to sing," Ethan said. I giggled. He's not the best of singers.

"Yes, you. And Esther, too. Now hurry."

Would the whole day be us hurrying meals between everything we did? I hoped so. I felt very important. Especially with my secret.

I decided over sliced turkey and gravy that I would not tell Father and Mother a thing. I would just appear on stage as Hildy. Grace could sit with Nonny in the front row. Mother would be near the side to prompt* people if they forgot what to say. Father would stand in the back to make sure everyone spoke loud enough. Only Ethan would see me backstage, dressed as the lead.

After eating we hurried to the Tabernacle. Already a large crowd was forming. Mother pushed us past people who milled about*. They shouted congratulations to each other like it was because of them Utah was now a state.

When I walked through the big wooden doors into the Tabernacle, my mouth dropped open. I had never seen it decorated like this before.

"It's splendid," Mother whispered.

A flag, bigger than any I had ever seen in my life, stretched across the ceiling. A thrill went through me to see that there were forty-five stars sewn onto the sea of blue.

"Oh, Esther, Ethan."

Mother stopped directing us to the front where the children were long enough to clutch her hands up to her chin.

"Look at that star," Ethan said. The forty-fifth star seemed to glow. Why, the forty-fifth star *was* all light. Electric lights shone through a hole cut in the cloth of the flag.

The sight made a lump come up in my throat. "We're a part," I said. "We're truly a part of the United States." For some reason tears sprang to my eyes. Maybe it was Mother's reaction, the way she stood there, so respectful. Maybe it was the excitement I felt now getting all mixed up with what was going to happen tonight. Maybe it was just seeing the flag.

Ethan pointed to the organ, its copper-colored pipes stretching high toward the ceiling. There hung the the words "Welcome Utah." A large star with a beehive in the center of it was also suspended from the ceiling. These things were lit up with lights. Below the word *Utah* hung a golden *1896*. The sight of it all made me draw in a deep breath. And I wasn't even acting.

A woman with a red, white, and blue banner strung across her shoulder came forward. She held a bundle of tiny flags. "Will you be singing?"

I nodded. So did Ethan. Even he was quiet. Maybe he felt the same way Mother and I did.

"Well, hurry to the front. Find a seat. And take these flags. I hope you remember all the words to the song." She pushed Ethan and me forward, and we went to find a place to sit. Scattered around us were people from our neighborhood and some children that we knew from church. I saw Grace from far across the room and waved at her. She gave me a small smile.

We practiced our songs a couple more times; then President Woodruff came into the room. Some people stood when they saw the prophet. So did I. Two men helped him walk to his seat. I could tell by looking at him that he wasn't feeling well. Again, tears came to my eyes at seeing a prophet of God so close.

You're a big baby, Esther Wall, I thought. Crying all the day long.

Thousands pressed forward to listen to the program that finally began a little after noon.

Lots of people spoke. The National Guard fired a forty-five-round salute.* Even though they were a mile away, we still heard the booming. The best part of the program, though, was when we sang. There were at least a thousand children. Each of us held a little flag and we waved them in time to the music. We sang three songs: "The Star-Spangled Banner," "America," and the new song that had been written especially for today, "Utah, We Love Thee."

At the end of the celebration, when everyone was leaving, Grace signaled to me.

"Esther," she said. "We've got to talk."

CHAPTER NINE

How The Wind Blew

I followed Grace outside the Tabernacle. There were so many people that I worried we might get lost.

"Meet us on the corner of Brigham Street," Mother said. She smiled at me, her small smile. I couldn't quite meet her eyes. Did she know that I had been thinking of getting the part of Hildy? It was true that Grace worried about the play, but it was also true that I really wanted the lead.

Grace and I clutched hands and pushed through the crowds.

"There's a quiet spot over under that tree," I said. I pointed to a slender maple, bare of its leaves.

We hurried in that direction, but it was like being swept along by rushing water. We went this way and that, shoved by people trying to get home and keep on celebrating. Finally we were near the tree. I looked at my friend.

Grace took both my hands in hers. "Esther, I can't do it."

"Grace . . ."

"No, I'm serious. I just can't. I'm so frightened that my hands are shaking." She held her hands out to me. She was right. They were both shaking. I took hold of them.

I remembered Mother's smile. "Grace," I said, "you *can* do it."

"I can't."

"We've worked so hard. You know the lines. You haven't forgotten them, have you?"

Grace shook her head no. "I still remember them all."

"Once you get going on stage, doesn't all the fear go away?"

Grace thought. "Yes, I think it does."

"I'm sure you can do it," I said. "I'm sure you can. Mother says all that fear changes to energy for her. She thinks it helps her to do a better job. I bet that will happen to you."

"I don't think so. I'm too scared."

"You can do it." I said. "I know you can play the part of Hildy. You know everything there is to know. And my mother has great faith in you."

"She does?"

"Yes. I do, too. I really believe you will make a great Hildy."

Grace looked at the toes of her black shoes. "You really think so, don't you?"

"I do."

Grace threw her arms around me so tightly that I thought she might squeeze the breath out of me. "I'll try, then. If anyone knows about acting, you do."

"Well," I said. I kicked the toe of my boot in the hard dirt.

"Thank you, Esther. You are a true friend." Grace turned to go meet her mother in the Tabernacle. I watched her get lost in the crowd.

"There goes my part," I said to the maple. "I was Hildy for almost a day."

I thought of Mother again. Truly she would be surprised if I showed up on the stage. It probably wouldn't be a happy surprise for her, either.

I felt a little sad as I walked away from the Tabernacle and past the Temple to where I was to meet my family. People still pushed this way and that, but things were beginning to calm down.

"Esther." It was Ethan calling. "Esther. We're over here." I saw my brother waving. Nonny sat close to him. Mother and Father waited for me, too. Mother smiled when I waved.

"Thank goodness," I said. I would never want to disappoint Mother. I liked her smile too much.

Once at home we only had time to eat and then run out the door again. This time we headed for the play. Everyone seemed excited. Even Abigail. She was coming to the play with her two sisters because Robert, the Wind, was her cousin. It was the first time I ever saw her actually smiling, though she did stop when she caught me looking at her.

In the theater, Nonny and I went to our usual places. Mother went to encourage the players. Father greeted people at the door. Ethan peeked out between the curtains. About half the chairs were full by then.

"He's probably gone to tell Grace how many people are out here," I said to Nonny. "I better go check on her. I'll be right back."

I made my way through the stage doors and into the area where everybody waited to be announced.

The Wind was very busy stuffing more stuffing into his gray suit. The trees were actually losing paper leaves. The salesman kept making sure his suitcase would open, so he could show his wares.* I was glad to see he had it with him. Mother ran here and there.

I searched for Grace. At last I found her, practically wrapped in a red velvet curtain, because she was so nervous.

I came up behind her. "Grace," I said into her ear.

"Oh, Esther. You've come. I prayed so hard that you would come."

"I can't do the part, Grace. You have to do it. There's no time for me to change into costume."

Even now I could hear Father joking with the audience.

"I know," said Grace. "I just wanted to see you. I knew I'd do okay if I saw my best friend before I went on to perform."

I hugged Grace close. How could Mother have known that I would like Grace so much? Tutoring her had not only given her a friend. It had given one to me.

"I'll be watching for you. I'm sitting in my same place. Nonny is there, too."

Now Mother's voice filled the room. Grace hurried to her spot. I went back to sit out front with Nonny.

I got to my place right when the curtains were opening. There was a brief hesitation from backstage, and then Grace appeared. She walked calmly to her mark and in a clear loud voice began her lines.

It was Ethan who messed up.

He blew on stage at the same time as the salesman. My face turned red for my brother. He was early.

"Care to see my wares?" the salesman asked.

Ethan stared out at the audience.

The salesman leaned a little closer to my brother.

"Care to see my wares?" he asked again.

Ethan didn't answer.

"Oh no, Nonny," I whispered. "Ethan has forgotten his lines."

Grace moved close to the trunk and peered in. "I've only a dollar," she said. It was Ethan's line. "My brother Thomas, though," Grace pulled Ethan around her in a small circle, "he might be interested in this sundial."

Ethan stared now into the suitcase.

The salesman smiled, grateful someone was saying someone's lines.

"What's that, Hildy?" Ethan suddenly said. His back was to the audience. The only reason I heard him was because he had wandered to my side of the stage.

"Wrong line," I said to Nonny.

"Wrong line, Ethan," Nonny shouted from beside me. "You're supposed to say 'This sundial has an unusual look.'" She talked slowly, but her voice was loud and very clear.

I stared at Nonny. The people in the audience around us began to buzz with whispers.

"Nonny," I said. "You spoke."

From the back of the room I heard Father. "Was that you, Nonny?"

Ethan peered off the stage. "Nonny," he said.

"What's going on?" someone behind me asked.

"She's not spoken in months," I said.

Father came running down the aisle. Mother came from out of the place where she prompted people.

"I can't believe it," Father said. "I cannot believe it."

Mother hugged Nonny around the neck.

Grace called from the stage, "Oh, Esther. She's better."

"This is the first time the lady has spoken in a long time," I heard someone tell someone else.

"Why, it's a miracle," said another.

Grace started clapping for Nonny then, and in only a few seconds the whole audience joined in. Tears fell from my eyes because I felt so happy. I hugged Nonny close and even hugged Ethan.

We might have continued our family celebration if someone hadn't called out in a very loud voice. "Let's get going. People want to see this show."

It was Nonny. Her talking was slow, but she was talking.

CHAPTER TEN

Nonny

After the play, Mother and Father went dancing at the Salt Lake Theater. It was the Inaugural Ball. We didn't expect them home until late.

"I have no idea what happened to me," Ethan said. He and Nonny and I sat near the fireplace in the dining room, popping corn.

"I know what happened to you," I said. "You got scared. You were so scared you couldn't even think."

Ethan smiled a little. I could see he was still embarrassed.

"Don't worry," I said. "It's happened to everyone. Except me, of course."

Ethan rolled his eyes.

"Well, it hasn't. Nonny, do you want more popcorn?"

Nonny shook her head. All of her movements were slow.

"Grace gave a good performance," I said. I felt very pleased for my friend. Not only had she saved Ethan at the beginning, but she never stumbled, never missed a line, and when she cried, I could see tears.

"Yes, she did," Nonny said.

I looked up at my grandmother. It was still unusual to hear her voice. I stood and gave her a hug. Her shoulders felt very thin. But her voice was the same.

"Nonny," said Ethan. "We're glad you're back."

"I've been here the whole time," Nonny said. "I was just a little lost. I couldn't find things."

"What things?" I asked.

"My voice, for one."

It was slow talking to Nonny, but hearing her made my heart warm.

We finished our popcorn and I put things away. Ethan pushed Nonny toward her room at the back of the house.

Popcorn Popper

"Wait, Ethan, Nonny," I said. I was at the end of the hall, looking out the stained-glass window to the street. The light of the lamp pushed through the glass barely, just showing the colors there.

"I have something to say, before you retire for the night." It was a line from the play. I wasn't quite ready to go to bed myself. I wanted a few more minutes with my family.

"What's that, Hildy?" Ethan said.

"You all are so important to me. No matter how

the wind may blow," I said, and Nonny joined in on the line.

I ran down the hall to my grandmother.

"Oh, Nonny," I said, putting my arms around her neck, "Grace was good tonight, and so was Ethan once he remembered what he was supposed to say. But you gave the best performance of all."

"My sweet girl," Nonny said. "It was you who had faith in me. This whole family never gave up."

"How could we?"

"I'm old."

"Nonny," Ethan knelt in front of her. "It wouldn't be the same without you." He kissed both her hands.

"You speak, Nonny. Thanks be to heaven, you speak," I said, remembering Father's play again.

"Hildy?" Ethan asked.

"And you move," I shouted, throwing my arms up in praise.

Nonny laughed and clapped.

GLOSSARY
In Esther's own words

au revoir (pg. 7)—Au revoir is French for good-bye.

constitution (pg. 23)—When Mother said to Ethan that gulping his food was bad for his constitution, she meant it wasn't healthy for his body.

flounced (pg. 5)—When I flounced from the room it means I left quickly and in a huff. That Ethan, he surely does try to bother me.

forty-five-round salute (pg. 57)—When the National Guard fired a forty-five-round salute they were helping us to celebrate. Big guns were shot, sometimes even cannons are used. At this celebration there was a shot fired for every star on the flag, including our forty-fifth one.

hearth (pg. 50)—The hearth is where the fire burns. Another name for it is the fireplace.

Manifesto (pg. 24)—After the Manifesto was issued, it was against the law for men to have more than one wife. Some people still continued to practice polygamy. If the men chose to do so, they were jailed or they went into hiding. Grace's father decided to hide so he wouldn't be jailed.

milled about (pg. 55)—Lots of people milled about or stood at the Tabernacle.

Mormon tea (pg. 25)—Mormon tea was a hot drink we enjoyed that wasn't made from harmful ingredients.

muff (pg. 52)—A muff is a covering for your hands. It's usually made of soft fur, and in the winter it's nice to hold a heated potato inside your muff, because that way your hands can stay really warm.

ornate (pg. 28)—Ornate means really fancy.

portrait (pg. 43)—Before there were cameras, people had their portraits painted. A portrait is just a painting of someone's face.

project (pg. 11)—I helped Grace to learn how to project her voice. That means I helped her to learn how to talk loud enough that lots of people could hear her.

prompt (pg. 54)—Mother's job in the play was to prompt people to say their lines if they forgot them. She would whisper a couple of words to help remind the speaker what he was supposed to say. She really needed to help Ethan at the end, but Nonny did it, instead.

quibbling (pg. 45)—When mother told Ethan and me to stop quibbling, she wanted us to stop arguing.

reprimand (pg. 35)—A reprimand is a correction. When Father reprimanded me he was telling me to behave. It was very embarrassing for me.

schoolmarm (pg. 28)—A schoolmarm is a school teacher.

started (pg. 19)—When I say Nonny started, it means that I surprised her.

stays (pg. 16)—When I asked Grace if she was cinched too tightly, I wondered if the stays of her dress had been pulled too hard. Stays are bones that are sewn into undergarments called corsets. They are a little like a girdle, in that they make a person's waist smaller than it really is. Lots of times girls were dressed just like their mothers. It could be very uncomfortable wearing corsets. Be glad you don't have to.

Sunday liquor laws (pg. 44)—There used to be laws in Utah that people were not to drink on the Sabbath. Those were called Sunday liquor laws. If you got caught drinking or drunk outside, you could go to jail.

wares (pg. 14)—When the salesman brought out his wares that meant he was showing the things he had to sell.

wraps (pg. 60)—Clothing like a shawl or coat you wear when it is cold outside.

What Really Happened

For many years the territory of Utah was separate from the rest of the United States. The Mormons had left much persecution behind and settled the desert so they could worship God as they wanted. But things began to change. Gold was discovered in California and the railroad went through Utah. This brought many non-Mormons to the Utah territory. They settled in the area. Eventually the people wanted Utah to be made a state. The rest of the country wanted Utah to be Americanized. That means they wanted the Latter-day Saints in Utah to be more like they were.

After time, changes were made in Utah, and on January 4, 1896, Grover Cleveland, the President of the United States signed the statehood proclamation for Utah to become the forty-fifth state. Celebrations took place all that weekend, with Inauguration Day occurring on January 6.

The celebrations that you read about in this book happened just the way you read them. Only the characters have been made up. There really wasn't an Esther Wall or an Ethan or even a Nonny.

About the Author

Carol Lynch Williams is surrounded by girls!

Having four daughters and growing up with her grandmother and sister, Samantha (who is now a mother of three daughters), it's no wonder Carol enjoys writing for girls.

She loves to write almost as much as she loves spending time with her family. Living in Mapleton, Utah, Carol shares her time between "wife stuff," writing, and home-schooling.

A modern "Latter-day Daughter," Carol grew up in Florida, where she and her sister joined the LDS Church when Carol was seventeen.

After serving a mission to teach deaf people in North Carolina, Carol moved to Utah, where she became an interpreter (and children's book writer).

She still finds time to teach sign language, teach Relief Society and Primary, and write between six and fourteen books each year. She also has two books published with Delacorte Press, and a third due out this fall.

Carol fills her family's life with her youthful sense of humor, great story-telling, "and the yummiest bread a mom can bake!" She is our role model, teacher, and best friend.

—Love, Drew
(Carol's husband)

From *Violet's Garden*
Another exciting new title in
The Latter-day Daughters Series

Mattie, I can hardly tell you of the terror. Everyone, even Ma, was screaming. Pa's face turned ashen grey. I pulled on Romie's lead as best I could, but she stood frozen and could not be coaxed forward. Pa yelled, "Hold her, Vi! Hold her, or we'll go over the side."

"We're all going to die," Rose cried.

"Stop it, girl," Pa said. "We surely will if these oxen are spooked again. Now stay quiet."

More about
The Latter-day Daughters Series

After reading Esther's story be sure to enjoy the other books in the Latter-day Daughters Series. They are about girls just like you who lived in other times and places. Read about Clarissa, who had to leave everything to come to America; Anna, who was a special friend to the Prophet Joseph Smith; Sarah, who plays matchmaker for her father; Violet, who tries to make the desert blossom; Maren, who cared for Joseph and Emma Smith's children; and Ellie who celebrated the 50th year the Pioneers entered the Salt Lake Valley.

Watch for many more stories of adventure, laughter, tears, and fun. They have been written just for you!

The Latter-day Daughters Series